*For Christopher and **every** kid not afraid to*

us their Imagination.

PROTECTO the GUARDIAN ROBOT
Defender from Monsters
A Christopher Smith story

It was 8:30pm. Dinner was delicious, and all of the chores were completed.

Homework was checked and playtime was awesome as always.

"Time for bed Mr."

Christopher's mom said this as he was headed to his room, with his new toy robot in

hand. He had just brushed his teeth and now it was time to relax & sleep.

"Say your prayers and get some rest." She went to kiss him on his head before she

tucked him in. "I love you."

"I LOVE YOU *TEWWW!!!*"

PROTECTO the GUARDIAN ROBOT
Defender from Monsters
A Christopher Smith story

Now, because he is the King of Everything, (*as seen in his 1ˢᵗ book*)

even his dreams are AMAZING! As he starts to dream, the scene shifts from his

bedroom to his *SECRET LABORATORY* hidden somewhere between under his bed

and the hall bathroom! It's a huge room full of scientific marvels far beyond the

minds of regular almost 9-year-olds.

With cape and crown on, we find

Christopher in front of his ALPHAMEGA computer screen receiving a threatening

message!

The image on the monitor shows a frightening figure with the

look of BAD NEWS in his eyes!

PROTECTO the GUARDIAN ROBOT
Defender from Monsters
A Christopher Smith story

PROTECTO the GUARDIAN ROBOT
Defender from Monsters
A Christopher Smith story

"Attention Christopher Smith! The *SO- CALLED* King of

Everything! I am *Frightmare, the Nighttime Monster*! I come vowing to **INVADE** the

world at midnight tonight while everyone is asleep! With my **Dream-Cannon**, I will

blast them all with a

FRIGHT INDUCER so they will stay asleep and I can terrorize their dreams

FOREVER!!!!!! HAHAHAHAHA!

I will enter your world through **YOUR** bedroom closet!

You and your puny planet are _DOOMED!_"

PROTECTO the GUARDIAN ROBOT
Defender from Monsters
A Christopher Smith story

PROTECTO the GUARDIAN ROBOT
Defender from Monsters
A Christopher Smith story

Christopher looked worried! He had never faced a monster like this before! Would he

be able to stop him and his sinister plan? How much time did he have before

Frightmare would make his move?

How could he protect the people of earth that were helplessly

sleeping, completely unaware of the danger?

That's when Christopher's worried look turned from a frown to a

HAPPY CIRCUS CLOWN!!!

PROTECTO the GUARDIAN ROBOT
Defender from Monsters
A Christopher Smith story

Christopher realized 3 things from the message:

1. He had to act fast if he planned on saving the world from the **DIABOLICAL**

    scheme of **FRIGHTMARE!**

2. *This had to be the <u>DUMBEST</u> MONSTER in the history of MONSTERS for*

    TELLING Christopher ALL of his plans BEFORE he carried them out!

3. *YOU NEVER <u>EVER</u> TELL ALL OF YOUR PLANS! What a <u>DOPE!</u>*

    Without a moment to spare, he dashes off to his Research

    & Development room to begin his ingenious plan of saving

    everyone!

PROTECTO the GUARDIAN ROBOT
Defender from Monsters
A Christopher Smith story

PROTECTO the GUARDIAN ROBOT
Defender from Monsters
A Christopher Smith story

Without hesitation, he reaches for items that will pass for legs, long and flexible.

Circuits, wires, transistors! He then grabs his toolbox to create what appears to be

the housing unit for whatever he's building. Wielding torch, screwdriver, what looks

like arms and finally what can only be described as, **THE HEAD**! It seems to have

some sort of light structure by the top of it. Working feverishly, he twists, turns,

repositions, and adjusts his unknown creation.

WHAT IS IT???

He looks at the time. It's 11:45pm! He only has 15 minutes

before FRIGHTMARE arrives!

PROTECTO the GUARDIAN ROBOT
Defender from Monsters
A Christopher Smith story

PROTECTO the GUARDIAN ROBOT
Defender from Monsters
A Christopher Smith story

Meanwhile, back in the lair of Frightmare, with 1 finger up like some dictator he

looks out into his domain with a defiant smirk on his face ! *"Now, NOW* is the time!

When the clock strikes 12 midnight, I will invade the sleeping world and they will

NEVER awaken! A new age of **NIGHTMARES by FRIGHTMARE** will begin!

With my Dream-Cannon, the planet will be powerless defend themselves!

AH! 3 minutes to go! NOTHING can stop me now!"

HAHAHAHAHA!

PROTECTO the GUARDIAN ROBOT
Defender from Monsters
A Christopher Smith story

PROTECTO the GUARDIAN ROBOT
Defender from Monsters
A Christopher Smith story

Back in his R&D room, cape & crown off to be able to work faster,

Christopher stands in front of his latest creation, Brand NEW and shiny! It is TALL,

looks robotic and like it could stop a TANK! Or at least an attack from some SILLY OL

Monster! "Perfect! With just a few minutes to spare! I shall call

you

PROTECTO! The Guardian Robot! Defender from

Monsters!"

With a confident smile Christopher moves Protecto from the

R& D room into position in his bedroom. " As soon as I hit this button, you will be

fully automated with 1 job. PROTECTING people from Nighttime

Monsters!"

PROTECTO the GUARDIAN ROBOT
Defender from Monsters
A Christopher Smith story

Frightmare has now approached the other side of the closet, Dream Cannon in hand! How he got there is anyone's guess. He snickers aloud and says "Look out world, I, Frightmare am coming to invade your dreams!

PREPARE to be Terrorized forever!

HAHAHAHAHAH! "

He pushes the door open, about to step out into the room.

He's about to get a VERY BIG surprise!

PROTECTO the GUARDIAN ROBOT
Defender from Monsters
A Christopher Smith story

PROTECTO the GUARDIAN ROBOT
Defender from Monsters
A Christopher Smith story

When the clock strikes midnight, the closet door opens and Frightmare jumps out

ready to blast everyone with his Dream Cannon. He is ready to place the planet into a

state for **FOREVER-SLEEP**! But, before he can, **PROTECTO** uses his Secret Weapon,

the antenna like thing on his head to **BLAST** Frightmare to Smithereens! " **Take that**

Frightmare," says Christopher! "You just got hit with the **DAY-RAY!** The ONE thing

night-time monsters can't take. DAYLIGHT!

Your evil plan never even got started thanks to

PROTECTO! The Guardian Robot! Defender from Monsters!"

PROTECTO the GUARDIAN ROBOT
Defender from Monsters
A Christopher Smith story

PROTECTO the GUARDIAN ROBOT
Defender from Monsters
A Christopher Smith story

The world was saved! All the sleeping people could continue to rest, not knowing

that it was the quick thinking of the King of Everything and his creation Protecto

that saved the night **AND** day!

And just like that, Christopher wakes up! WOW! What a dream he thought! He

looked at his toy robot, still in his hand. He smiled and got up to go get some

breakfast. As he walked past his closet door he didn't bother to look down. He told

his parents all about the dream he had, and they both shook their heads and

laughed!

What he was NOT aware of, is that, in his room, by his closet door, there was

"SOMETHING" purple in a small puddle of Goo.

Beside it, a beat up, broken gun like device. **PERHAPS**, it wasn't a dream after all...

THE END!

PROTECTO the GUARDIAN ROBOT
Defender from Monsters
A Christopher Smith story

This is the **end** of the Christopher Smith story line. I hope you have enjoyed both books.

This is the **BEGINNING** of the NEW Nighttime Hero